Noel
First Christmas

Story by Elizabeth Marsh
Illustrated by Anna Abramskaya

I dedicate this book to:
Gloria and Anna for helping make my dream come true. Your dedication to your craft is priceless. Thank you from the bottom of my heart.
And to
My mother and father
Thank you for being truly amazing people. You have inspired me to never give up.
I love you.

On a cold and snowy Christmas Eve, there was a Noble Fir tree named Noel who lived at a Christmas tree lot.

She always dreamed about going home with a family for Christmas.

When Noel was a baby tree, a snowstorm caused another tree to fall on her. Once the other tree was removed her top had grown crooked.

Because Noel looked different, the other trees made fun of her. People would walk through the lot laughing and making jokes. No one wanted to buy Noel for Christmas.

At last, a family drove into the lot. A little boy and his father got out of the car. "Hey Dad" the boy shouted "Look at that tree. It has a crooked top. Let's go somewhere else."

"Hold on" The father replied, "You wanted a different tree this year. I think this tree is perfect." Overhearing this, the lot attendant insisted they take Noel home.

Noel couldn't believe it. Finally, she was going to be a Christmas tree. When they got home, the father dragged Noel gently into the house, and set her up in the living room.

The son started putting lights on her branches. There were red, green, yellow, and blue lights. Some lights blinked and some didn't. There were red and white candy canes, purple unicorns and a beautiful ribbon on top.

Noel was covered with twinkling lights and
dozens of different ornaments. Noel was proud.

After everyone went to bed, Noel awoke to a noise.
Something was tapping on the roof. Suddenly, in a big puff of soot Santa
Claus appeared right in front of the fireplace.

Noel couldn't believe her eyes. Santa was standing right in front of her. Chucking to himself, Santa walked over and opened his bag of toys.

Presents leaped from Santa's bag
to hide under Noel's branches.
Gifts scrambled up the fireplace
to dive into the stockings. Noel
shook with excitement.

Munching on a cookie, Santa wrote a thank you note for the snacks, and with a wink of his eye he disappeared up the chimney.

Noel heard him get into his sleigh and dash away. She felt
very special with those presents underneath her.

Noel was so excited for morning to come
that she couldn't sleep the rest of the night.

The next morning, the family pranced
and danced around her. They laughed
and had a merry time.

Noel wished for Christmas day to last forever!

On a frosty morning a few days after New Year's, the family took all the lights and ornaments off of Noel and planted her in the front yard.

For the next week, Noel was so depressed that she didn't talk to any of the trees around her. Finally one day, one of the other trees asked why she was so sad.

Noel said "The family doesn't want me anymore. I will never be a Christmas tree again."

"No, no not true" replied the other trees, "The family loves us. They decorate us every year." Noel smiled, "Really, I will be decorate again next year! I can hardly wait!"

Noel's crooked top didn't matter anymore. She was going to be a Christmas tree forever.

About the Author

This is Elizabeth's first children's book. She plans on writing many more, and loves getting inspired by what's around her. Elizabeth grew up in a small town in Washington State, where she still resides. In her spare time, Elizabeth enjoys cooking and camping with her friends and family.

Smiles are free, pass them along!

Made in the USA
San Bernardino, CA
16 December 2013